D0390027

The Doll with the Yellow Star

YONA ZELDIS McDONOUGH

illustrated by

KIMBERLY BULCKEN ROOT

Henry Holt and Company
New York

Henry Holt and Company, LLC
Publishers since 1866
175 Fifth Avenue
New York, New York 10010
www.henryholt.com

Library of Congress Cataloging-in-Publication Data
McDonough, Yona Zeldis.
The doll with the yellow star / Yona Zeldis McDonough; illustrated by Kimberly
Bulcken Root.—1st ed.
p.   cm.
Summary: When France falls to Germany at the start of World War II,
eight-year-old Claudine must leave her beloved parents and friends to stay
with relatives in America, accompanied by her doll, Violette.
ISBN-13: 978-0-8050-6337-0
ISBN-10: 0-8050-6337-4
1. Holocaust, Jewish (1939–1945)—Juvenile fiction.
[1. Holocaust, Jewish (1939–1945)—Fiction.   2. Dolls—Fiction.
3. Jews—Fiction.   4. Paris (France)—History—1940–1944—Fiction.
5. France—History—20th century—Fiction.]
I. Root, Kimberly Bulcken, ill.   II. Title.
PZ7.M15655 Dp 2003   [Fic]—21   2002027554

First Edition—2005 / Designed by Meredith Pratt
Printed in China

1 3 5 7 9 10 8 6 4 2

35757722 7/07

For Susan Schnur, whose words led the way
— Y. Z. M.

Contents

Happy Birthday

What *is* that brushing gently against her cheek?
Fur? Feathers? Wisps of a cloud that slipped in
through the bedroom window? No, it's just
Maman's soft hair, falling over her face as she leans
down to kiss Claudine's cheek. "Time to wake up,
darling." She smiles. "Happy birthday!"

Claudine opens her eyes and stretches. The
morning sunlight pours in through the dotted Swiss
curtains that Maman is now pulling open; it illu-
minates the pink-and-green flowered wallpaper,
woven rug, and small bentwood rocker that sits in
a corner of the room.

Claudine pushes the covers aside and feels
around on the floor near her bed for her slippers.

"Hurry. You don't want to be late," Maman

urges, and then she goes downstairs. Claudine dresses quickly and follows her. The table is set with the good damask tablecloth and the china they use when company comes for dinner. There is a small crystal vase near Claudine's plate that holds flowers Papa must have picked from the small garden out back.

Claudine sits down. Her bowl is already filled with steamed milk, and her sliced *baguette*—the long, wand-shaped loaf of bread—is spread with butter. This is itself a special treat because, ever since the war began, food has been in short supply. Claudine is very hungry, but before she can begin eating she is stopped by a large cardboard box that dominates the table. Claudine is eight today. And there is a present after all. Maman and Papa had said they weren't sure they would be able to buy her a present this year. It was because of the war— again. But somehow, despite their predictions, they have managed to get her one.

Eagerly she reaches for it and unties the red

grosgrain ribbon. Pulling away at the sheets of white tissue, Claudine can't wait to see what is tucked inside. When the last piece of crumpled tissue paper has dropped to the floor, she holds her new treasure in her hands. It is a doll. A beautiful doll.

"Oh, Maman! Papa!" cries Claudine. "Thank you so much!" Her parents beam. Breakfast is temporarily forgotten as Claudine runs her fingers over the doll's wavy auburn hair, smooth pink cheeks, and dimpled chin. She looks into the doll's eyes, which are made of amber glass and fall shut when her body is tilted back.

Then there are her clothes. A red wool felt cape worn over a plaid pinafore. Her linen blouse has a round collar and three pearlized buttons down its front. Her stockings are crocheted silk, and her black shoes are made of real leather. "I've never seen such a doll," says Claudine, and indeed, she had not.

Of course, Claudine had other dolls. There was Nanette, a baby doll in booties and a bonnet, who held a glass bottle in her hand. And there were Olga and Elsa, two very grown-up lady dolls, who wore long dresses, high-buttoned shoes, and big, fashionable hats. But this doll is neither a grown-up nor a baby. She is a girl just about Claudine's age. Someone to play with, share with, confide in—a friend as much as a toy. Claudine tucks her in the crook of her elbow. The fit is perfect.

"Hello, Violette," she murmurs. Her parents look at each other, slightly confused.

"What's that, my sweet?" Papa asks.

"Violette," Claudine repeats. "That's her name."

Claudine immediately sets herself the task of making Violette feel at home. The large cardboard box in which she arrived looks like it could be useful. Flipped over, the box makes a perfect bed. Its lid becomes a canopy, held up by four wooden dowels taken from Papa's toolbox. Maman's contribution—a pile of worn but pretty lace-edged handkerchiefs—is also pressed into service. Claudine uses some of them to cover the canopy and make a dust ruffle. Others become sheets. An old pincushion is turned into a soft pillow, and two damask dinner napkins stitched together and stuffed with some old bits of batting are a warm and cozy doll quilt. Maman offers Claudine an empty round box with a gold-and-white design, which, when paired with a matching rectangular soapbox, functions as a smart set of luggage.

That gives Claudine another idea: doll clothes to put in the luggage. Claudine asks Maman to look through her fabric scraps. Maman patiently shows her how to measure and trace a pattern, to cut, baste, and finally sew a garment.

"Your stitches are so tiny," Claudine complains. By comparison, Claudine's look large and crude.

"Practice will make them perfect," Maman says. "Here, why don't you try again?"

Claudine picks up the needle and begins to sew. After about half an hour, her hand feels cramped and her eyes are tired. She looks critically at the work she has just finished. A little better, she decides, surveying a seam.

"What do you think?" She brings it into the kitchen for her mother to see. Claudine's mother looks at the seam and then at her daughter.

"I think Violette is lucky to have you taking care of her."

———❧❧❧———

In the weeks that follow, Violette joins Claudine on her trips around the neighborhood and the city. With one of Maman's checkered kitchen towels to cushion her, she rides in the wicker basket that Maman sometimes uses at the grocer. That way she can go to school, where she waits patiently on a shelf in the cloakroom until recess, when she is taken down and admired greatly by the other girls in the class. She also accompanies Claudine to the houses of her friends Simone and Odile, and to the parks and public gardens where they play. Simone and Odile bring their dolls along, too, and the three girls invent elaborate dramas for them to act out. Bushes and trees become castles and dungeons; ordinary dolls are cast as princesses, witches, and fairies. A fallen leaf turns into a magic carpet; a gray stone, into a crystal ball.

"Your stories are always the best," says Simone.

Odile agrees. Claudine is proud. Although she does not tell her friends, it is something about Violette that brings the stories out of her.

—❧❧❧—

On Sundays, Claudine's family often takes the train to the country to visit her grandmother. Using a footstool covered with a large doily, Claudine's grandmother hosts a doll tea party, serving tiny jam-filled pastries made from leftover scraps of dough on the hand-painted china doll dishes that had been hers as a girl. Claudine carefully pours the tea into the cup and holds it to Violette's lips. Violette says nothing but seems to smile in a very contented way. "We'll always have fun," Claudine murmurs as she balances the doll on her lap. "Because we'll always be together."

Trouble Comes Home

Something is wrong. Claudine tells Violette about it, although she is sure that the doll has noticed it, too. It has to do with the hushed conversations between Papa and Maman that stop suddenly when Claudine enters the room, and with the anxious glances they keep exchanging when they think she isn't looking. The newspapers that are quickly put away whenever she comes near. And the urgent whispers into the black telephone that stands on a table in the hallway, whispers that end abruptly when Papa or Maman catches sight of her.

Finally all the secrecy ends when they sit Claudine down on the sofa in the parlor and tell her about the yellow star. Claudine already knows

about Adolf Hitler, the terrible tyrant who holds
Germany in his thrall and who declared war on
France. She had seen the headlines in the morning
papers and heard the news on the radio. His evil
armies had made their way relentlessly west, and
they marched right into France. Now France is an
occupied country, and the citizens have to obey
Hitler's laws. One of these laws says that all Jews
must wear a yellow Star of David on their coats
when they leave home. And because Claudine's
family is Jewish, they, too, will have to wear the
stars.

Claudine is stunned. She has never thought too
much about what it means to be Jewish. She knows
that on certain holidays—Rosh Hashanah, Yom
Kippur—she puts on her good velvet dress and
goes with her parents to synagogue. Some Fridays
they go for dinner to her other grandmother's, the one
who lives in Paris. The table holds candlesticks and
silver cups filled with wine; her grandmother says a

Hebrew blessing over the candles and serves a meal that always includes a braided golden challah bread. But none of that seems so odd.

The neighborhood where Claudine and her family make their home is one where Jews and Christians live together. At Hanukkah, Maman brings out a brass menorah and lights the candles, one each night for eight nights. There are crisp potato pancakes with applesauce for supper, and afterward, Grandmère's special, crunchy, twice-baked cookies for dessert. The cookies are filled with walnuts and raisins and dusted with cinnamon sugar. At Christmas, Claudine is invited to Simone's house, where she exchanges presents with her friend and gets to taste the *bûche de Noël* that Simone's mother prepares. There has been no reason to feel ashamed or frightened that she is a Jew, until now.

Claudine watches quietly as Maman carefully traces and cuts the stars from the yellow cloth. First she sews a star onto the breast pocket of Papa's tweed jacket. She sews another onto her own camel coat, and finally, she sews a slightly smaller one onto Claudine's navy-blue wool duffel coat.

"I hate that star. I won't wear it," Claudine declares, breaking the silence. Maman doesn't answer. She puts the sewing things away and goes into the kitchen to start dinner. They are having stew, and soon the warm, enticing aroma wafts its way into the room where Claudine sits, not moving. She sees her coat hanging on the hook near the door. The star glows hot and ugly; she longs to rip it off. Instead, she turns the coat inside out, so she won't have to see it.

⟨◦/◦/◦⟩

The next day, Claudine wears the star in public for the first time. Although no one appears to react or even notice, Claudine is unable to forget she has it on for a single second. Her face burns pink with shame. She clutches Violette to her tightly, because she doesn't want to cry. Violette does not have a star. When Claudine returns home, she throws her coat on the floor instead of hanging it up as she usually does. Then she asks Maman for the sewing box.

"What for, Claudine?" Maman wants to know. "Are you going to make your doll a new dress?"

"Violette needs a star," Claudine answers defiantly, as if expecting to be challenged. "She wants to wear one, too."

"Yes, that's a good idea," murmurs Maman. She helps Claudine make a tiny yellow star, which they position on the front of the doll's red cape. "No, not there," says Claudine. They move the star higher and lower, left and right, and all over the red cloth. They even try it on the back, but still Claudine is not satisfied. Finally, she remembers turning her own coat inside out last night, when she saw it defaced by the star for the first time. Claudine takes the star and places it just inside the cape's opening. Maman's careful training has paid off, and Claudine is able to sew it neatly onto the red felt by herself.

"There," says Claudine with grim satisfaction. "That way, she can be the one to choose to let it show."

——⸱⸱⸱——

Maman and Papa do not share Claudine's indignation over the star. They are more concerned with other things, like the food shortage all over the city. Maman has to wait in line for hours at the greengrocer, the butcher, the cheese shop, and the baker to buy food. And what poor food it is! The carrots soft and wizened, the potatoes and apples half rotted. Bread that tastes like it has been baked with sand instead of flour. Some days no cheese or meat at all, only rinds, which Maman scrapes down as best she can, and bones, from which she makes a thin, watery soup.

Papa has been forced to leave his job at the university, where he has taught French literature for so many years. The children who came to see

Maman in the afternoons for piano lessons have found reasons why they cannot come anymore. Suddenly, Claudine is not welcome at Simone's house, nor at Odile's. They can only see each other at school, but soon Maman and Papa tell her that she may no longer attend school. No more lessons from the strict Mademoiselle Rousseau; no more running in the yard during recess or giggling with the others. And all because she is a Jew. When she learns this, Claudine takes Violette into her arms and presses her face against the doll's soft hair. How can these terrible things be happening to them? And why?

———✍———

The worst comes one quiet morning when Claudine goes downstairs for breakfast. She sees the grave faces of her parents and knows that there is yet more bad news. Things are growing increasingly dangerous for the Jews, not only of France but all over Europe. That's why Maman and Papa want to send her away, to her aunt and uncle in America.

America! Aside from the occasional night with a friend or one of her grandmothers, Claudine has never been apart from her parents before. Surely Maman and Papa will come, too?

"Not now," says Maman sadly. "I wish we could."

"Maybe later, if we can," adds Papa.

"I want to be with you," says Claudine tearfully.

"Leaving France now is almost impossible," Maman says. "It's a miracle that we were able to arrange safe passage for you."

"But why can't you come with me?"

"We only had enough luck for one miracle," says Papa quietly. "Not three."

Claudine looks from one worried face to the other. Then she rushes from the room, climbs the stairs, and gets back into her bed. She doesn't want to eat breakfast, put on her clothes, face the day. She wants to go under the covers and pretend this is all a bad dream. She'll close her eyes, wait here for a while. Then she'll get up, go downstairs again,

and this time there won't
be any talk of wars or of
trips to America. Maman
and Papa will
smile when
they see her.
Things will be
the way they were
before.

Claudine remains in
bed for what seems like
a long time. With her eyes
closed, she can hear her par-
ents moving around downstairs. She tracks their
movements by the sounds they make. Maman is in
the kitchen, doing the dishes; she recognizes the
rush of the running water. Papa is in the study; she
heard the door open and then close. Neither one of
them mounts the stairs to find her. Claudine opens
her eyes. Her stomach growls. She looks at
Violette, who is lying in the box that is now a bed.

It was only a few months ago that she received the doll, made the bed in which she would sleep. And yet it feels like years.

Claudine gets out of bed and reaches for her. Against her pink cheek, Violette's lashes curve thick and dark. "I think we ought to go downstairs now," she says, holding the doll tightly in her arms. "Don't you?"

Quietly, she descends the stairs and waits in the doorway of the kitchen until Maman turns to face her.

"Are you ready for breakfast?" Maman asks.

"Yes," says Claudine. "I'm ready now."

Saying Good-bye

Preparations for Claudine's departure begin almost at once. There is packing, though not very much of that, for she won't be able to bring many bags with her. "Aunt Adele and Uncle Gus will buy you what you need," Maman promises. So Claudine can take only two dresses, two skirts, and two blouses. A sweater, a coat, some underthings and socks. A nightgown. No books, no toys, no dolls. Not even Violette? "I won't go without her," protests Claudine. Her parents exchange worried looks and finally relent. Violette may go, but only Violette — not her bed, trunks, or any of the other things Claudine has made or improvised for her. "We'll take care of everything while you're away," says Maman.

"It's not for long," says Papa. "As soon as it's safe again, you can come home."

But didn't they tell her they would come to America if they could? Both of these things can't be true at the same time.

———◦/◦/◦———

Two days before she is scheduled to leave Paris, Claudine tells her parents that she wants to say good-bye to Simone and Odile. Even though she has not seen them for a while, Claudine doesn't believe they don't like her anymore.

"No, you can't do that," Papa says. His voice sounds angry. Also frightened.

"Why not?"

"Your going has to be kept a secret. The fewer people who know about it, the better."

"Why?" Claudine knows she is being difficult, but she doesn't care.

"Because there's a war going on."

Claudine repeats this last sentence along with him in her mind. It's easy; she's heard it so often lately.

Although she doesn't actually disobey Papa, she gets her coat and heads for the door. She tells herself that she's just taking a short walk around the neighborhood before she must leave it. It doesn't mean anything if she happens to stroll past Odile's house. Still, her heart is beating hard when she turns the corner of the street where Odile lives. She knows she's doing something wrong, but she's here already. Although it's daytime, the shutters are latched tightly, as if no one is home. She stares at the house for a few minutes. There are geraniums still in the window boxes, and the brass doorknob is polished to a gleaming brightness. Yet for all that, the house feels abandoned, and it unsettles her.

At Simone's, the shutters are open. Claudine knows where her friend's window is, and she glances up toward it, hoping to catch a glimpse of her. The window is empty though, and a lace curtain flutters weakly in the breeze. Downstairs, she sees Simone's father standing in front of the door.

She wants to wave but something stops her. It is the expression on his face — he is frowning. Can he see the yellow star from where he stands? Claudine looks down and hurries away.

———※※※———

Finally, everything is ready. Maman has the ticket and all the papers — passport, the letter from Aunt Adele — that Claudine needs. The small bag is packed. Claudine will make the journey with Mademoiselle LeBlanc and several other French children who are on their way to safety across the Atlantic. First they must go to the port at Le Havre. There they will wait — in hiding — until they are ready to board the ship. This is her last night at home with Maman and Papa for a long time. Tomorrow she will have to say good-bye to her pink-and-green room, the flower-filled garden behind the house. At least Violette can come along. She is somewhat comforted by the thought.

In the morning, Maman doesn't have to wake Claudine, who gets up when the sky is still dark.

She has no appetite but eats a few bites anyway, if only to ease the worried look on Maman's face. Maman has not eaten much either and soon moves the dishes aside. She sits down next to Claudine, who is holding Violette on her lap.

"Here," says Maman, pulling something out of her apron pocket. "I thought you would want to take this." She gives Claudine a small photograph. There are Maman and Papa, holding hands and looking very happy. Maman wears a long white dress and grasps a bouquet. Papa wears a dark suit and elegant hat. Their wedding picture.

Claudine feels the top of Violette's head pressing against the underside of her chin as she studies the picture. She knows that Violette is studying it, too.

"Look at it when you feel lonely," Maman

tells her. "And when you think about us, remember that Papa and I will be thinking about you. All the time."

Claudine wants to find a safe place to put the picture. Her own pocket is too easily opened; her valise seems too big. Then she has an idea. "I need scissors," she tells her mother, and she goes to get a pair. Claudine carefully trims the photo down so that it is little more than the two smiling faces. She slips the tiny square she has made into the pocket of Violette's pinafore and sews it shut. "Now I know it will be all right," she says. And for a moment, she believes it.

Crossing the Ocean

The journey to America will take nearly three weeks. The ship cannot go directly to New York but must stop at several other destinations first. Claudine feels lonely just thinking about it.

Once she is actually on board, it is hard not to be frightened, confused, and sad. The other children seem as bewildered as she is. When the sea is rough and choppy, they stay belowdecks, clutching their stomachs and calling for their mothers. Often they cry out from bad dreams in the night; Claudine can hear their plaintive voices, along with the soothing one of Mademoiselle LeBlanc as she tries to comfort them.

During the day, Mademoiselle LeBlanc conducts lessons: history, geography, arithmetic, poetry, and writing. Claudine tries to pay attention. When she was in school in Paris, poetry was her favorite subject, and last year she won a beautiful ribbon for her excellence in memorization. She stood up on a stage in front of the whole school to recite a sonnet and receive her award. But here on board the ship, she finds it hard to concentrate on schoolwork of any kind. Instead, her mind wanders back to Paris. Where are her parents now? What are they doing? Have they kept their promise about her room? Did Papa remember to bring her bicycle into the cellar so it wouldn't rust? And what about Odile and Simone? Have they found out she has left the country? Do they miss her?

Claudine is very grateful to have Violette, for the doll makes her feel less alone. When the weather is good and the ocean calm, she brings her on deck, where they stand together and look at the vast gray expanse. Claudine stares out past the railing. All she can think about is what she left behind and the puzzle of what lies ahead. But after a couple of days, she notices that there is another girl who often stands at the railing at the same time. The girl has two long blond braids and a fringe of blond across her forehead. She is always holding a large toy monkey in her arms. The monkey has brown fur and a cream-colored face with black buttons for eyes. He wears a black collar around his neck. Following Claudine's gaze, the girl holds the monkey out toward her.

"Would you like to see him? His name is Jax."

"He's very nice." Claudine touches the monkey's face.

"I like your doll," the girl adds shyly.

"This is Violette. And I'm Claudine."

"Mathilde," says the other girl. "Maybe we could play together while we're on the boat. With Jax and Violette."

"That would be fun," agrees Claudine, smiling for the first time since she said good-bye to her parents. "Are you going to New York City, too?"

"Only to dock," says Mathilde. "After that I go

to a place called California. I have to take a train."

"What about your mother and father?" Claudine asks.

"My father died. It's just my mother, my big sister, and me." Mathilde looks sad, but then she brightens. "And Jax, of course."

"Of course," says Claudine.

———◦/◦/◦———

It turns out the two girls lived not far from each other in Paris. Mathilde, too, was forced to wear the awful yellow star. Claudine shows her the lining of Violette's cape. "I wanted to sew mine inside like that. Only my mother wouldn't let me." Clearly Mathilde is impressed by Claudine's attempted resistance.

Mathilde quickly becomes Claudine's new best friend. They sit together during the lessons and invent games with Violette and Jax in the afternoons. Now that she has someone to play with, Claudine finds that she actually likes some aspects of being on a ship. The salt smell of the breeze, for instance, as it rises up to meet her in the mornings. The fantastic, ever-changing shapes of the clouds as they go scudding across the sky. She and Mathilde begin to explore the ship, which offers many opportunities for new and exciting games. There are barrels and ropes; portholes and ladders.

One afternoon they discover a rowboat, complete with oars and life preservers, on one of the lower decks. This prompts Claudine to think of a game. Violette and Jax are stowaways on a big luxury liner; they use the rowboat to glide off in the middle of the night to an enchanted island. Claudine asks Mademoiselle LeBlanc if she can borrow some colored pencils and uses them to draw a very detailed map of where the island is located.

"Did you think of this all by yourself?"

Mathilde asks. "Or did you read about it some-where?"

"It's my own idea," Claudine says.

"You should write it down," Mathilde says. "Like a story in a book."

───❊❊❊───

Late one afternoon, as the sun seems to sink slowly into the water, Claudine and Mathilde descend several narrow flights of stairs. They have never been down this far before, and they are excited. They prowl around for a few minutes and soon find themselves standing in front of a strange-looking door. It is wide and squat; Claudine can easily imagine that it is the portal to some secret netherworld, hidden at the bottom of the ship. Maybe there are mermaids living here. Or sea monsters. She tries the doorknob. It is locked, but she spies a key suspended from a brass hook on the wall. Unfortunately, the hook is too high for her to reach.

"Give me a boost," she says to Mathilde.

"Do you think we should?" Mathilde asks.

"We won't touch anything. We'll just look."

"I'm not sure . . .," Mathilde says.

"Oh, come on," urges Claudine. "I just have to know what's in there!"

Mathilde gives in and helps Claudine reach the key. Once the key is in her hand, Claudine unlocks the door. Inside there is a furnace filled with glowing coals. She gestures for Mathilde to follow. Together, the two girls explore the room. It doesn't take long because there isn't much to see. How disappointing. They back out of the room, and Claudine locks the door again. After returning the key to its hook, she and Mathilde go upstairs. They might have even forgotten about the whole thing had not Mademoiselle LeBlanc noticed the soot on their faces, clothing, and shoes. "How did you get so dirty?" she asks. "Where have you been?"

Reluctantly, Claudine tells the story. They're in trouble now, she thinks, reaching for Mathilde's hand. But to her surprise, Mademoiselle LeBlanc is less angry than alarmed.

"That was very dangerous. The furnace is hot. You children could have been badly burned. Promise me you'll never go down there again." She pulls both girls close and wraps her arms around them. Claudine thinks of the coals. They didn't look dangerous at all; in fact, they looked quite ordinary, even a bit dull. But then there were other things that seemed dull or ordinary and turned out to be dangerous. Words in the newspaper. Or a scrap of yellow cloth, cut into the shape of a star.

Safe Harbor

The long journey across the ocean is coming to an end. Mathilde and Claudine point to the tall, proud statue in the distance. "Lady Liberty," explains Mademoiselle LeBlanc. "A gift from the French people to the Americans." Knowing this lifts Claudine's spirits a bit, and she looks forward to seeing the statue get larger as they approach New York City, where they are soon to dock. Claudine is eager to arrive. Although she has never met Aunt Adele, she hopes that Maman's sister will be as loving and kind as Maman herself. And she has American cousins: Marc, who is ten, and Audrey, who is six. Maybe they will grow to be friends.

But she is very sad to have to say good-bye to Mathilde. The two girls exchange addresses and promise to write. Then they hug tightly. Claudine wishes they were going to be together. There have been so many good-byes. They stand on the deck as the ship approaches the shoreline. Claudine's bag is packed and ready; Violette is lying on the bed in her cabin. Soon Claudine will go down and fetch them both. The sky over New York City is wide and blue; the tall buildings rise up into it. Today is a hopeful day. Maybe landing here will be the start of something good.

She is about to ask Mathilde if she feels that way too, when suddenly a shout interrupts her thoughts. At first, the word *fire* means nothing to her—she speaks no English. But the cry is repeated in French—*au secours!*—and then she understands. There is a lot of frantic shouting now. Also running. Claudine stands frozen at the ship's brass railing until Mademoiselle LeBlanc grabs her arm and hurries her along.

"Up there," she shouts. "Let's go!" Claudine has

never heard Mademoiselle sound so alarmed before, and she feels her own fear rising up like the great flame she imagines is burning somewhere out of sight. Claudine follows her quickly. Mademoiselle gathers more of their little group and soon they are all together, watching as the smoke pours out of the cabin windows.

"It must have started in the furnace room belowdecks," Mademoiselle LeBlanc is saying to another grown-up. Claudine looks around sharply at these words; she remembers when she and Mathilde found the secret door and the key. . . . Was that where the fire started? Could they have been responsible? But they hadn't touched anything. And besides, that was days ago. She wants to ask just to make sure, but is distracted by the black coils of smoke that mount quickly toward the sky and fill it with acrid, dark clouds. She has never seen such clouds, and they terrify her.

"Don't be frightened," says Mademoiselle

LeBlanc, in an effort to soothe the children, some of whom are crying. In truth, she sounds frightened herself. The boat seems to pick up speed as it approaches the shore. Claudine hears the loud wails of sirens; fire trucks are already gathered and waiting for them. Mademoiselle is busy counting off the children on her fingers. "All here," she says with a sigh, and closes her eyes briefly. Claudine sees Mathilde standing a few feet away. She is holding Jax. Claudine realizes with horror that her own arms are empty—Violette is not in them. The doll is waiting for Claudine to rescue her. She must go down to her cabin to get Violette, she must! She tugs on Mademoiselle's arm to get her attention.

"There's something I need down below," she tells her. "I have to go now."

"But that's where the fire started!" protests Mademoiselle. "There's so much smoke—it's much too dangerous." She looks searchingly at Claudine's face and adds, "What did you leave behind?"

"My doll," says Claudine in a low voice, feeling embarrassed by the admission. Still, she must save Violette, so she goes on, "My parents gave her to me. She's very special."

"Ah!" is all Mademoiselle says, but Claudine can see she understands. "Don't worry," continues Mademoiselle. "They'll put the fire out before we dock, and we can get her later. I'll go with you myself." She puts a hand on Claudine's shoulder and draws her close.

———❦❦❦———

Despite Mademoiselle's encouraging words, Claudine is unable to retrieve Violette or her bag from below the deck. There is so much noise and confusion when the boat docks, with firemen and police officers running every which way and yelling at the top of their voices. They direct people off the boat and hurry them through customs and immigration. Claudine can't get anywhere near the stairs again, nor does she get a chance to say a proper

good-bye to Mathilde, who is led away by a very large, loud woman in a polka-dot dress. All she can see are Mathilde's blond braids flopping around as she hurries to keep pace with her companion.

But Claudine has no time to think about that either. Almost immediately, she is found by Aunt Adele and Uncle Gus, who have come to meet the boat and are frantic when they learn about the fire.

"We'll contact the ship's crew in the morning," soothes Aunt Adele, steering Claudine away from the crowds, toward the car that will take them home. "I'm sure your things will turn up, and Uncle Gus can drive in tomorrow to get them." Claudine herself is not at all sure that this will happen but says nothing. Instead, she keeps her eyes closed during most of the trip to Long Island, where her aunt and uncle live. As the noise of the cars, buses, and trucks gives way to sounds of birds and children calling to one another, Claudine cannot get Violette out of her mind. If only she had not left her in the cabin. If only she had brought her on deck, as she had so many times before! But it is useless to think about that. Maybe Aunt Adele is right. Tomorrow they will call, and someone will find Violette and return her to Claudine. She opens her eyes and looks around at the streets and roads and houses of what will be her new home—America.

"Here we are!" calls out Aunt Adele as the car pulls into a driveway on a pleasant, tree-lined street. Compared to the house in Paris, her new home is in the country. Lawns, shrubs, and flowers are all around. Across the road, a horse grazes in an open meadow. The car stops and Claudine gets out. There in the open doorway of the house stand a girl and a boy. Her cousins, Audrey and Marc.

"Come and say hello," Aunt Adele says, extending her hand to Claudine.

In America

Claudine tries hard to be happy in America. Her aunt and uncle are kind and loving. Little Audrey worships her and spends her time making cards and posters for Claudine. Even Marc is friendly enough; he shows her how to play American board games like Monopoly. Claudine has her own room, on the top floor of the house. While it is not the pretty pink-and-green room she was used to in Paris, she has to admit it is very nice. There is an oval rag rug, white chenille bedspread, and curtains Aunt Adele sewed herself, using an old dress that had a wonderful pattern of big parasols, some open and some shut.

Even with numerous telephone calls to the shipping agent's office in New York City, Claudine's things do not turn up after the fire. Her aunt and uncle take her shopping right away at a large store where they buy her a brand-new coat, skirts, blouses, and a cardigan for school, as well as a taffeta party dress. And because she is so sad about losing Violette, they offer to buy her a doll.

Claudine cannot bear the idea of having a new doll. She wants and longs only for Violette. "Are you sure?" her aunt and uncle ask again.

"Yes, I'm sure," she says, shaking her head as they stand before the plate glass window of the toy store. Through the window she can see a wall of alluring dolls lined up in a neat row. Next to the dolls are handsome doll trunks and clothes and real furniture, like armchairs, a dining table, and a kitchen set—icebox, sink, and stove, with what look like real copper pots on its burners. Claudine looks away.

"You can play with my dollies," says Audrey in French, shyly slipping her hand into Claudine's.

"I'll let you have any one you want." Claudine takes her cousin's hand and doesn't let go.

———◈◈◈———

Gradually, Claudine grows accustomed to her new life. With the help of her uncle and aunt, she learns to speak some English, though the words feel clumsy on her tongue. Aunt Adele suggests that she read some of Audrey's books, the ones that have a single word—*cat, ball, hen*—with a corresponding picture on each page. Claudine rejects the books as too babyish. But after studying them for a while, she has to admit that they do help. Soon she is able to talk to Audrey in English and tease Marc back when he teases her. There is a new school and new friends, who love her French accent and ask her lots of questions about Paris. "Does everyone wear a beret?" asks one girl. "And do people really carry loaves of bread under their arms?" The silly questions cheer Claudine up, if only a little. No one here says anything about being Jewish, and for this

Claudine is grateful. When she first arrived and asked if she had to wear the yellow star, Aunt Adele wrapped her in her arms and said, "Not here, my darling. Thank God, not here."

Claudine still thinks about her parents and misses them terribly. Once in a while, she gets a letter on thin, blue paper from Papa. When it arrives, she tears it open and immediately reads it two or three times over. Then she puts it away carefully in a wooden cigar box Uncle Gus has given her and slips the box under the bed. Although Papa does not actually say so, Claudine can tell that he is not with Maman. This worries Claudine; it is important for her to think of them together, like in the wedding picture Maman gave her. She believes that together, they will be safe. She also notices that the postmarks keep changing: first Paris, then Nice, then Paris again, then Amsterdam. Papa seems to be traveling a lot. She wonders if Maman is traveling, too.

After Claudine has been in America for a couple

of months, the letters stop coming. Without them, the time seems to go slower and slower. Claudine plays little games with herself while waiting for the mailman to come up the street. If he steps on more than five cracks on the sidewalk, no letter will come. But if Claudine sees two white cars pass the house before the mailman arrives, then surely he'll have a letter from Papa. Three white cars mean a letter from Maman. None of this turns out to be true, of course. Claudine changes the rules of the game: She waits for blue cars, a red truck, a black dog, a spotted cat.

A letter comes from Mathilde. Her friend is having a difficult time in California. She has not heard from her mother or sister and doesn't know what happened to them. Claudine knows just how Mathilde feels. She takes out the letters she does have from Papa and reads them again, hunting for a clue about what might have happened, but there is nothing.

⚞◦/◦/◦⚟

Soon it is her birthday again, her first birthday in America. Her aunt and uncle throw her a birthday party with games like pin the tail on the donkey, musical chairs, and charades. Afterward, there is a cake — Aunt Adele has been saving their rations of butter and sugar for weeks to make it. Uncle Gus dons a tall black hat and red satin cape. He performs a magic show in the living room, and all the girls gasp with wonder at his clever tricks. Aunt Adele puts big silver hoops on her ears and ties a silk scarf around her head. Seated at the kitchen table, with the lights out and the curtains drawn, she pretends to be a Gypsy fortune-teller. "I see good things ahead for you," she tells Claudine as she peers into her open palm. "Really? What do you see?" Claudine asks. She doesn't believe Aunt Adele can read the future, but she goes along with the game.

"A reunion," says Aunt Adele. "And it will come very soon." Claudine touches the oval locket her aunt and uncle have given her as a birthday gift. Inside are two tiny pictures, one of Papa and the other of Maman. Not the wedding picture, which is tucked in Violette's pocket, wherever *that* is, but another one her aunt had in a photograph album. The locket makes a tiny click when Claudine snaps it shut. She holds it tightly in her hand, hoping all the while that her aunt's prediction will come true.

Still Waiting

Claudine's birthday has come and gone with no word from Maman and Papa. She starts paying more attention to what she hears on the radio or can read in the newspaper. Although some of the words are big and unfamiliar, her English is getting better, and this new language is slowly becoming her own. The Allied nations — France, England, America — are fighting hard against the Nazis. The Nazis have many tanks and powerful weapons. Claudine wants to believe that the Allies will win and the Nazis will be defeated.

Claudine can sense that her aunt and uncle are worried. Not that they say anything directly to her, but they start turning off the radio or putting away the newspapers when she comes into the room. She remembers how her own parents used to do these things back when they were all together in Paris. It seems like so long ago.

———◦/◦/◦———

The weeks and months pass, sometimes quickly, other times with a maddening slowness. Claudine watches two more birthdays go by—her tenth and eleventh—without hearing a word from her parents.

One afternoon, shortly after the celebration for Claudine's eleventh birthday, she and Audrey are curled up together on the sofa in the den. The day is rainy, and the window outside is streaked with little rivulets of water.

"Do you think they're still alive?" Audrey asks innocently.

Claudine does not have to ask who Audrey means. She puts down the book she has been reading aloud to her cousin; her English is good enough for her to do that now. Claudine pauses. Sometimes she has wondered the same thing, but she has never permitted herself to say it out loud.

"Of course they are," she says with a confidence she does not feel. "You'll meet them one day. They'll come here to get me. You'll see."

They go back to their reading, but now Claudine can't seem to concentrate. Audrey suggests a board game or cards. Claudine shakes her head no and goes up to her room.

Once she is alone, Claudine replays the conversation in her mind. She knows she sounded very sure of herself when she answered Audrey. But inside she is not so sure. Why hasn't she heard from them? Are they really all right?

Later that day, she confronts her aunt directly. "Do you think they're still alive?" she asks, echoing Audrey's question. Aunt Adele is standing at the stove; she looks up quickly from the soup she is stirring. She doesn't say anything for a moment, and Claudine feels a flash of fear. "Do you?" she repeats, more insistently this time.

"We are praying all the time," her aunt says finally.

After this conversation, Claudine begins to experi-
ence the sense of unease she felt back in France
during those months and weeks before she was sent
away. Her dreams are clouded and filled with menace.
Two or three times they force her awake. Once
though, she has a good dream, about a unicorn and
a princess and a rose-colored castle hidden in the
clouds. When she wakes up, the dream stays with
her all morning long, and she wishes she could hold
on to it forever. It is like a story she wants to read
again and again.

Stories. Her friends—Simone, Odile, and later
Mathilde—used to praise the ones she made up.
Isn't the dream just another story? Why can't she
write it down?

This idea makes her feel better than she has felt
in a long while. She begins to record her stories in
a notebook, giving them titles and chapters, just
as if they were in a real book. She writes slowly,

using her very best penmanship. Good thing Mademoiselle Rousseau was so strict. Claudine even draws a few pictures, which she plans to incorporate into her book. Although she tells no one her idea, she decides to present the book to Papa and Maman when she sees them again. It will be a gift that she has made during this long, hard separation. Maman was the one who always read to Claudine; won't she be proud to read stories Claudine herself has written?

Once upon a time, there was a beautiful mermaid who lived deep, deep under the ocean, writes Claudine. *Her red-gold hair was long and curling. The scales on her body were a shining green. They matched her eyes.* It all seems so real to Claudine as she writes; she can almost see the mermaid standing before her. *Though the water was clear and pale blue near the surface, down at the bottom it was inky and dark. The mermaid had to find her way through the dark; luckily, her glowing scales helped light her way.*

Sometimes Claudine's mind moves ahead faster

than her pencil can write, and she feels as if she has to hurry to keep up.

The mermaid was lonely. She wished she had someone to talk to, someone to play with. While she loved the many beautiful and shimmering fish and the other sea creatures, she wanted to find someone like her, another mermaid. She asked the giant gray whale if he could help her. But the whale just shook his great head sadly. He wished he could help her, but he didn't know of any other mermaids in the ocean. Maybe she should ask the octopus, the whale suggested. So the mermaid swam off in search of the octopus.

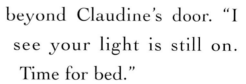

"Claudine?" calls Aunt Adele from the stairs beyond Claudine's door. "I see your light is still on. Time for bed."

"Just a minute, Aunt Adele," Claudine says, hurrying to finish her sentence before the thought slips away.

Together Again

One afternoon when Claudine, Marc, and Audrey are coming back from school, Claudine notices an unfamiliar car parked in the driveway of her aunt and uncle's house. At first she doesn't think much about it; some grown-up has come to visit, no doubt. All of a sudden she sees Aunt Adele's face peering anxiously out of the door.

"There you are," she says, as if Claudine has been gone for days, instead of the few hours she has been at school. "Finally!"

"Is something wrong?" Claudine asks, as she sets down her book bag in the hall the way her cousins do.

"No, nothing's wrong," says her aunt. But her voice sounds strange. "I have a surprise for you."

She leads Claudine into the kitchen, where a gray-haired man is seated at the table. He stands up when she walks in. It takes a few seconds for her to realize that the man is Papa.

"You came! You came!" cries Claudine, throwing her arms around him. Papa is here at last. She can hardly believe it. But how much he has changed. The hair, of course. It wasn't gray before. And he is so thin. When he crosses the kitchen to pour himself a cup of coffee, Claudine is shocked to see that his once springy step is now slowed by a slight limp. But his eyes are the same. Warm and loving, they never leave her face. Claudine stands in the kitchen, feeling almost foolish. She has thought about this moment for so long. Now it is here, and she can barely think of what to say. Even speaking French again feels strange to her.

"Where's Maman?" she finally says. Everything else can wait. "Is she coming soon?" But Papa's eyes film over. As the tears seep slowly down his cheeks and his shoulders tremble slightly, he turns

his face away. She is stunned. Never has she seen Papa cry, and she cannot imagine the thing that would cause him to do so. Unless. . . .

"It's Maman, isn't it?" she says, understanding everything all at once: why Papa looks so frail, the reason for his tears. "She's not coming, is she?" Claudine can hear panic in the shrill sound of her own voice. Papa looks at her again, his face still wet. He grasps her hands tightly.

"No," he whispers and pulls her to him.

⸻ ∽⊙∕⊙∕⊙∽ ⸻

Papa and Claudine remain with Aunt Adele and Uncle Gus for several more weeks. Spring has come to Long Island, and the war is finally over. "Too late for some," murmurs Aunt Adele, wiping her eyes quickly with her fingers.

Claudine doesn't have to ask what she means. But secretly she does not believe her mother is dead. Instead, she tells herself that Maman has gotten lost in all the confusion, just like Violette did. She is somewhere far away, but she is thinking of Claudine and Papa, trying to make her way back to them. Claudine begins writing a story about it in her notebook. She will not write the ending yet. When Maman comes—and although Claudine tells this to no one, she is convinced that Maman *will* come back—then she'll know how the story should turn out.

❦

Claudine and Papa wait until June, when school has finished for the year, before setting sail for Paris. Although she has missed her home, Claudine is surprised at how nervous the thought of returning makes her feel. So much will have changed. Maman is gone; what about everyone else? Her grandmothers? Papa has already told her that both of her grandmothers have died. But there are her friends. Will Odile and Simone be allowed to see her now? Will they want to? While Papa rests in the cabin below, Claudine stares at the waves as the questions swirl around in her head.

❦

The trip feels much shorter this time. For all her worrying, Claudine is anxious to be home. That's what France represents to her, home. But when they arrive, Claudine discovers with dismay that France without Maman is not the France she knew and loved. And the house in Paris is no longer the house she remembers. It, too, has suffered through the war.

Coming in the familiar door, she and Papa find so many of their things have been ruined or stolen. There is cracked china strewn all over the dining room; windows are broken everywhere; the furniture is either missing or upended, with cushions ripped open and mounds of feathers coating the floor. Papa explains gently how badly some people behave during a war: There is looting and vandalism. Maybe some Nazi soldiers were living in their house. Such things have been known to happen. Claudine says she understands; still, when she walks up the sticky stairs to her room, she cannot help but let out a great sob. Someone has done his best to shred the flowered wallpaper that Maman had chosen. Scrawled in horrible black letters is the word *juif*—Jew—on what is left of it. The curtains are in tatters, and the rocking chair is splintered beyond repair. Even the little bed that she made for Violette has been pushed rudely on its side in a corner. It is crushed and filthy now, the canopy covered in ashes.

When Claudine sees that, a sudden realization overtakes her. If this is what the Nazis have done to her home, she can only guess at what they might have done to her mother. As she absorbs the meaning of the dirty and disordered room, Claudine can no longer believe Maman is alive and will find her way back to them. Sitting on the debris-littered floor, Claudine begins to cry. All the tears she did not shed when Papa first told her Maman would not return come pouring out. She cries and cries. A sound on the stairs makes her look up; there is Papa in the doorway. He doesn't say anything, only gathers her in his arms until the weeping is done.

New House, New Home

After the shock has worn off, both Papa and Claudine realize that Paris is no longer a place where they can imagine themselves living and rebuilding their lives. In fact, once they have examined the extent of the damage to the house, they lose their desire to stay in France at all. Papa sells whatever has not been destroyed, and they set sail—once again—for America.

＊＊＊

Aunt Adele and Uncle Gus are happy to see them again. They tell Papa he and Claudine can stay as long as they like. But while Papa is grateful for their kindness, Long Island feels like the country, and Papa will never be a country person.

"It's too quiet" is what he says, but Aunt Adele and Uncle Gus exchange those worried looks Claudine has come to know well, the ones that say, "Uh-oh, trouble brewing." After lots of hushed talk, Claudine and Papa come to live in a place called Brooklyn.

Claudine feels so numb with grief that she does not care where she is. The last time she lived in America, she believed Maman would come back to her. Now that Claudine knows Maman never will, what does it matter where she lives?

In September, she will go to school, but until then the summer looms long and empty. She thinks of the notebook filled with her stories. She hasn't touched it since she accepted her mother's death. She just can't envision the proper ending for the last story in the book, and so it remains unfinished.

Papa, too, seems lost and wandering. Claudine pretends not to notice how his hands tremble when he holds a book or how frequently he buries his face in them, blotting out the light. Often, he spends the day in his bathrobe, not even bothering to get dressed.

Aunt Adele comes to visit, and Marc and Audrey join her. Even in her sadness, Claudine can dimly appreciate their kindness. Audrey makes her a paper doll with an entire wardrobe of clothing, and Marc decides he will teach her how to play softball. Claudine is not very interested at first, but after trying it for a while, she decides it is better to throw and catch a ball than to be alone with her thoughts. Aunt Adele talks to Papa who remains mostly silent. While Claudine washes her hands at the sink for lunch, she observes her father. He seems to look a little less gray and drawn today. Maybe something Aunt Adele said is helping.

⚘⚘⚘

The fall arrives, and the leaves begin to turn colors and drop from the trees. Claudine has a new school, and to her surprise, so does Papa. He will be teaching French in a Long Island high school where Aunt Adele knows the principal. Although Papa's English is far from perfect, he applies himself to improving. He and Claudine read English books at night, and he haltingly makes his way through the American newspapers.

Claudine can see that the new job is important to him. He shaves carefully and puts on a suit and tie. "I'll be home in time to pick you up," he promises before he leaves. Claudine nods and hugs him.

Although she cannot say why, the fact that Papa is feeling better allows Claudine to feel a little better, too. She begins to pay attention to Brooklyn, her new home. Here, the brick and brownstone houses have tall windows covered by lace curtains and fine front stoops that seem to be the perfect vantage point from which to sit and survey the world. There are some trees, though not that many, and lots of bustling little shops that Claudine likes to stop in: an Italian grocery with fat rounds of cheese and heavy ropes of garlic hanging from the ceiling; a Chinese laundry with neatly wrapped parcels lining the shelves. There is a bookshop with a soft sofa at the back where she can sit down and read; there is a pastry shop with cupcakes in its window—iced in pale pink, they are dusted with a delicate coat of sparkling sugar. When Papa buys a half-dozen, Claudine eats two on the way home. "Save some for me!" he jokes. Claudine is glad to see him smile.

On one of these walks, Claudine and Papa discover a shop that sells Jewish books and ceremonial objects. The small, cramped window is filled with menorahs and candlesticks, matzoh covers and yarmulkes. They stand there quietly looking in. Claudine remembers the brass menorah Maman used at Hanukkah; like so many things, it did not survive the war.

"Let's go inside," Papa says suddenly, as if he has read her thoughts. The woman behind the counter has white hair and tiny, rimless spectacles. She looks at Claudine and asks pleasantly if they need any help. "We're looking for a menorah," Papa says.

"Here's a nice wooden one," says the woman, bringing it down from a shelf. But wood is all wrong. They examine several more, finally selecting one that is not as fine as the one Claudine remembers, but at least it is made of brass. "Would you like some candlesticks as well?" the woman asks. "For the Shabbas candles?"

"Well," says Papa slowly, "Claudine has never lit the Shabbas candles before." It is true. While Claudine's grandmother, like so many Jewish women, had lit candles on Friday nights, Maman had not. Claudine had not learned how.

"I see." The woman looks from Papa's face back to Claudine's, as if she is trying very hard to understand the meaning behind the words.

"No one had a chance to show her how," Papa adds. There is a silence.

"Do you live nearby? Would you come again? On a Friday, just before closing time?" Claudine is puzzled, but the woman explains, "I live in the apartment upstairs. I'll show you how to light the candles, and I'll write down the blessing that goes with them. Would you like that?"

"Yes," says Claudine. "Yes, I would like that very much. Thank you."

Papa buys the menorah and a beautiful pair of silver candlesticks. The woman wraps them carefully in tissue paper and then places them in a bag. "Don't forget," she says as they leave. "Come back on Friday."

As they walk home together, Papa places his hand on Claudine's shoulder. "It seems to me that you're ready to light the candles now," he tells her. He is quiet for a moment and then says, "I think Maman would have thought so, too."

The Yellow Star

Claudine likes Brooklyn, even if the house she and Papa live in is not as well tended as the others on their street. The steps leading up to their front door are starting to crumble, and the tall wooden shutters are badly in need of paint; one is hanging by a single hinge. Inside, the rooms are rather bare, so the house doesn't feel like a home. Claudine suggests to Papa that they go looking for things that will fill it up.

"Things? What do you mean by things?" he asks.

"You know, Papa, rugs and lamps and pillows and pictures . . . ," she replies. The sort of things Maman liked, she thinks.

"Maybe that's a good idea." So Papa and

Claudine pack a wicker basket with a picnic lunch, get into the small silver car Papa recently bought to travel back and forth to his job, and begin their search. They drive to auctions outside the city. Claudine finds she enjoys the auctions. They are usually held in tents and you never know what magical thing you might uncover. Amid the furniture, rugs, paintings, and such, there are treasures to be found, like the miniature sailing ship miraculously suspended in a green glass bottle, or the clock whose face is painted to look like the rising moon.

"I like things that have a history," Papa tells Claudine, and he bids on both the bottle and the clock, which they put in the living room on the mantel, right next to a framed photograph of Maman. It chimes on the hour, a low, musical sound that Claudine loves to hear. She knows Maman would have loved it, too.

Now that Papa is more settled in his job, he seems to be putting down roots. He wants to buy furniture, like a wrought iron bed and an oak dresser with an oval mirror attached to its back for Claudine's room, and a big, green velvet sofa for the living room. Another time, he buys a pair of cobalt-blue ginger jar lamps and a needlepoint cushion with a design of violets worked into the center. Claudine wonders whether he remembers, as she does, how much Maman loved violets. And violet is the English translation of "Violette," her lost doll's name. Claudine aches inside when she thinks of everything that has been taken from her, but she says nothing to Papa. Instead, she lets herself be cheered by their house, which soon begins to look less empty and more welcoming. Papa even has the steps fixed and the shutters painted and rehung.

It is on one of these trips—the afternoon is especially beautiful, and they have the windows all rolled down—that they come to an old red barn that is having a sale.

"Funny that this one wasn't advertised," remarks Papa. "Should we stop? It doesn't look like they have too much."

"Oh, but look at that," says Claudine, pointing to a patchwork quilt appliquéd with large colorful butterflies. "That would look pretty on my bed."

So they get out of the car, and Claudine wanders around. The auction has just started, and Papa bids on the quilt and a few other things. Claudine doesn't pay a lot of attention because she is distracted by the mother sheep she finds on the other side of the barn. Two baby lambs are with her, and Claudine has such fun stroking their soft, wrinkled faces that she forgets about Papa. He finds her later, still petting the sheep, and holds up the quilt. "Voilà!" he says. "Do you like it?"

"Oh yes. Thank you, Papa!" Claudine pipes, jumping up from the grass and brushing off her skirt. "It's just beautiful." Then her eyes fall on something at Papa's feet.

"What's that?"

"An old blanket chest," he replies. "It's from the Pennsylvania Dutch country. I thought it would be good for your room. You could use it for your clothes and things." Claudine kneels to look more closely. The chest is painted with unusual colors, and the design is one of elaborately decorated hearts and flowers.

"I do like it, Papa," says Claudine. She kisses him. Then Papa loads it in the trunk of the car and they set out for home. Claudine holds the new quilt in her lap, watching the day gradually turn to evening. By the time they get home, it is dark.

―◦◦◦―

After Papa opens the door, Claudine goes upstairs to put the quilt on her bed. She is just smoothing the wrinkles down when Papa calls to her. She hurries downstairs again.

"Let's bring the chest up," he says. "Do you think you can help?"

"I'll try." She starts tugging on a corner. "It feels like there's something inside. We should empty it out first."

"Oh yes. The auctioneer said there were some

things in there. Books and linens and such," Papa says, and he pulls open the lid.

"Ugh, dust!" says Claudine, wrinkling her nose and coughing. But she peers inside anyway as Papa pulls out a long bolt of flowered chintz, a linen tablecloth, and a wad of napkins, all stained with rust.

"Say, what's this?" says Papa, his hand sunk down deep into the chest. "It feels like a doll." Claudine looks up. She has not had a doll since she lost Violette. At first she was afraid it would remind her too much of Maman and all that had happened. Later, she thought she was too old to ask for a doll, even though she secretly continued to want one. But if she and Papa were to find a doll by chance . . .

"Yes, here she is," announces Papa, pulling the doll, upside down, into the air. Claudine turns her upright and frowns. The doll is naked and very dirty, with auburn hair that is more of a tangle than anything else. Something sooty and gray covers her face. Under the thin film of dirt, her nose is chipped, and her bare, dirty toes are scuffed, as if she has been dragged along the floor. Papa peers over Claudine's shoulder. "Well, she is in pretty bad shape. Don't bother with her, *ma chérie*," he says. "We'll get you a new doll. We can go looking for one tomorrow."

But Claudine continues to study the doll, gently smoothing the hair away from her face. "I feel sorry for her. Maybe we could fix her up. Wash her, comb her hair." Even if she wouldn't actually *play* with a doll, this one arouses her pity.

"Well, why not?" agrees Papa, and he helps Claudine get a soft rag and a bowl of soapy water. They place the doll on the counter by the kitchen sink, and Claudine carefully washes away layers of dirt. It is only then that she notices something familiar about the doll's eyes. Claudine stares hard at her. Could it be . . . ?

"Papa," she says abruptly. "Papa, did we look

through everything in the blanket chest? Was there anything else?"

"We can check." Claudine hurries to the chest, digging her arms deep inside, rummaging around for what she scarcely believes might be there. First she pulls up some old kitchen towels, rolled into grimy balls, then another tablecloth. But what is that there, at the bottom? She yanks hard and finds herself holding a small white blouse, wrinkled and dirty, with missing buttons. She keeps digging and is finally rewarded with a red wool felt cape and a plaid pinafore. "Papa!" Claudine shouts. "Papa, look! These are Violette's things! The doll! It's Violette!"

"Are you sure?" asks Papa, doubtfully eyeing the rumpled, dirty clothes. Claudine takes the cape and folds back the opening. There, just inside, as she remembers it, is the yellow star.

"I'm sure!" she says and rushes back to the kitchen to see the brave little doll who has been

through so much sorrow before finding her way home. "We'll get you all fixed up again," she tells Violette, cradling the doll in her arms. Claudine forgets all about being too grown-up for dolls. "I'm sure there is a doll hospital in Brooklyn. We'll take you there, and you'll be as good as new. But there's one more thing."

Claudine sets down the doll and puts her fingers on the pocket of the pinafore, which is still sewn shut, as it has been since the day she and Maman were last together. "Papa, do you have any scissors?"

"Scissors?"

"For the pocket," she says.

"Here, use this." Papa hands her his red pocketknife and steadies her hand as she slices easily through the thread. Claudine slips a pinky inside the pocket. She can feel the tiny scrap, and yes, when she pulls it out, there are Maman and Papa, heads close together as they stand in the sunshine.

"Look, Papa!" cries Claudine as she hugs the doll tightly. "Here's the picture! Can you believe it? Violette has come back to us! She's come back!"

"Why, so she has, *ma petite*," says Papa, gazing down at his daughter and Violette. "So she has."

——◦/◦/◦——

Two weeks later, Claudine sits in her room, writing furiously in her notebook. Violette, freshly cleaned and restored, sits on a stool nearby. The man at the doll hospital was able to provide her with pearl buttons for her blouse, shoes, and socks. Her red felt cape, the blouse, and the pinafore have been cleaned and pressed. In Claudine's opinion, she looks older and wiser. If she could talk, she would have much to tell.

Claudine has many things she wants to share with Violette, too. The notebook filled with stories, for instance, and the ending to the last story, which has eluded her until now. Although Maman is not coming back, Violette did, and Claudine believes Maman was somehow responsible for this, though

she cannot exactly explain how. But with her pen
in hand and her doll at her side, Claudine sets to
work imagining the way in which that small miracle
might have happened.

She writes about the long trip on the boat, her
loneliness and fear, the fire in which
Violette was lost, seemingly forever.
As she keeps writing,
though, a very strange
thing happens. Claudine
finds herself wanting to
write about the good
things, too; the new
friend that she
made on board
the ship—she and
Mathilde have con-
tinued to write to
each other—as well
as the kindness of
her aunt, uncle, and

cousins, and indeed of this unfamiliar but accepting new land that has taken them in and offered them a safe home.

After a while, Claudine puts down the pen. She isn't nearly finished, but she needs to take a rest. Her eyes travel to the mantel, where the framed photograph of Maman holds the place of honor. In the picture, Maman is caught in the sunlight coming from the window near which she stands. Her hair, pinned up in braids that circle her forehead, gleams like a crown. Claudine continues to stare at the photograph for a long time. Finally, she looks back down at the paper and, with a quiet sense of peace that she believes is nothing less than her mother's blessing, once more begins to write.

Author's Note

The idea for *The Doll with the Yellow Star* first came to me after reading an article by Rabbi Susan Schnur in *Lilith* magazine describing the work of Trudie Strobel, a Holocaust survivor who lived through the terrible years of World War II and, as an adult, devised a unique way of dealing with the traumas of her past. "As a four-year-old in Russia, I had few comforts and playthings," said Strobel. "My prize possession was a beautiful bisque doll and I still remember the horror of it being torn away from me by a brutal Nazi guard on the transport to the camps." The article went on to describe how Strobel—aided and encouraged by a sensitive therapist—decided to re-create the lost childhood doll. Initially, Strobel intended only to make the doll she had lost. But then she found herself wanting to dress it the way women, and indeed all Jews, had been forced to dress—with the armband and the yellow star. She became increasingly drawn into the dark history of restrictive Jewish women's clothing, of which the star was only a late and vestigial remnant.

After completing the first doll, she was inspired to make another one, and another after that. Eventually, she made eleven, and her haunting, silent testimonials now reside at the Los Angeles Museum of the Holocaust.

Trudie Strobel's story stayed with me for years. I remained captivated by the idea of a little girl losing a doll — the symbol of childhood innocence — and by having that doll in some way restored. The brutality of World War II, a time when so much more than dolls was lost, is something that is hard for children — or anyone else, for that matter — to accept and understand. But in the symbol of the doll, I found something concrete and tangible to which a child could relate. It is my hope that the children who read this story will respond both to the sorrow of the lost doll and the joy of its recovery, even in the face of so much sadness.